ZZZzz

A Book of Sleep

By Il Sung Na

meadowside
CHILDREN'S BOOKS

When the sky grows dark,
and the moon glows bright,
everyone goes to sleep…

...apart from the staring owl.

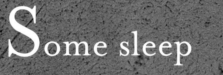

Some sleep

in peace and quiet,

Some make lots of noise
when they sleep.

Some sleep standing up,

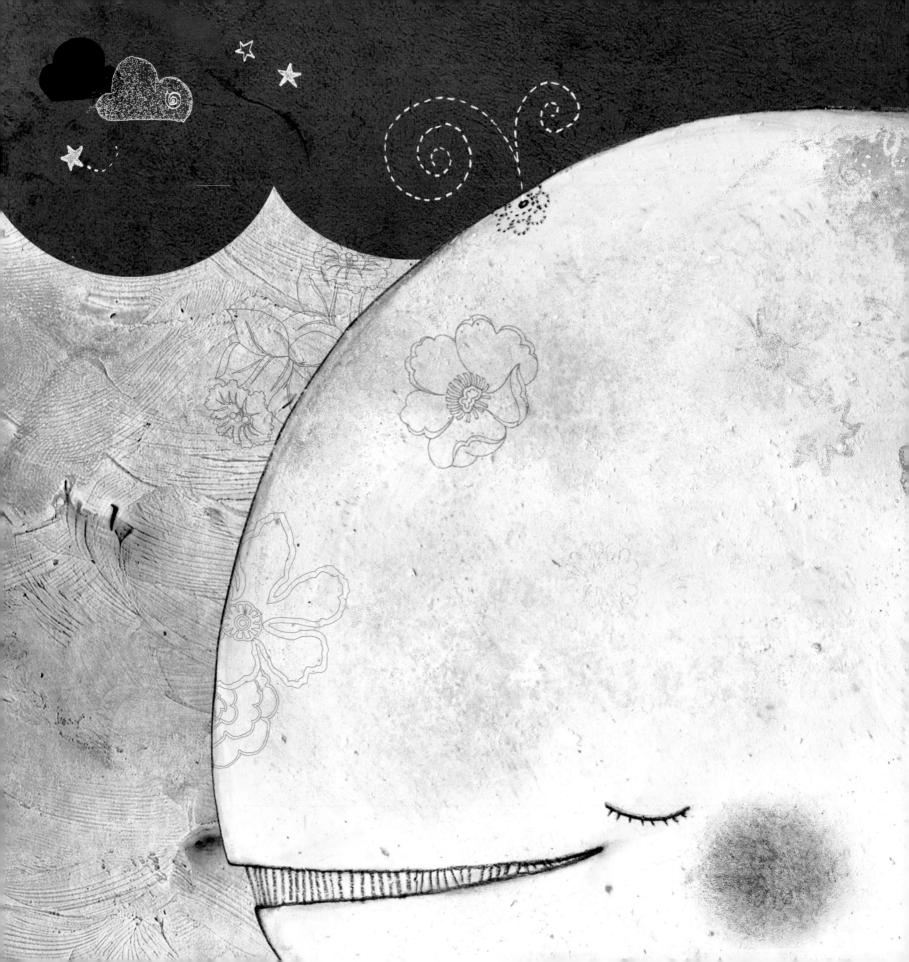

While some
sleep on the move!

Some sleep
with one eye open,

S ome sleep with both eyes open...

...they don't even blink!

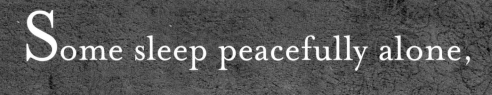

Some sleep peacefully alone,

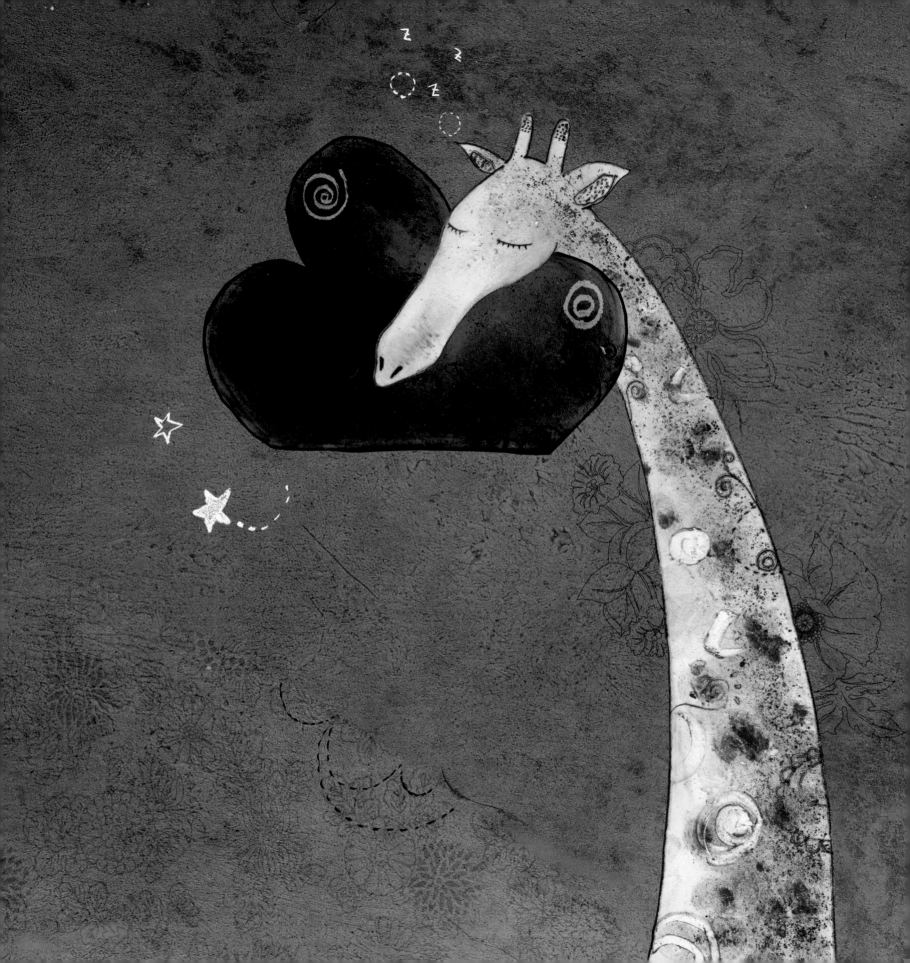

While others sleep all together,
huddled close at night.

But when the sky grows
bright and the sun
comes up…

…everyone wakes up!

Apart from the tired owl.

Z z z

For Mum and Dad

First published in 2007
by Meadowside Children's Books
185 Fleet Street London EC4A 2HS
www.meadowsidebooks.com

Illustrations © Il Sung Na 2007
The right of Il Sung Na to be identified as
the illustrator has been asserted by him in accordance
with the Copyright, Designs and Patents Act, 1988

A CIP catalogue record for this book
is available from the British Library
10 9 8 7 6 5 4 3 2 1
Printed in China